My Heart's
GARDEN

By
CHARITY RIOS

ILLUSTRATED BY

ANNA BRENNAN

Scripture quotations are from the NASB, NIV and ESV as indicated.

Scripture quotations taken from the New American Standard Bible® (NASB),
Copyright © 1960, 1962, 1963, 1968, 1971, 1972, 1973,
1975, 1977, 1995 by The Lockman Foundation
Used by permission. www.Lockman.org

Scripture quotations are from The ESV® Bible (The Holy Bible, English Standard Version®), copyright © 2001 by Crossway, a publishing ministry of Good News Publishers. Used by permission. All rights reserved.

Scriptures taken from the Holy Bible, New International Version®, NIV®. Copyright © 1973, 1978, 1984, 2011 by Biblica, Inc.™ Used by permission of Zondervan. All rights reserved worldwide. www.zondervan.com The "NIV" and "New International Version" are trademarks registered in the United States Patent and Trademark Office by Biblica, Inc.™

Endorsements for My Heart's Garden

"Our children are being bombarded with false and confusing messages about their identities and significance. My Heart's Garden provides an engaging and essential resource for parents, grandparents, educators, pastors and mentors to teach children how to connect to the Father heart of God and receive the truth about who they were created to be. If your children are struggling with anxiety, fear or insecurity, buy this book!"
-Dawna De Silva, Founder and Co Leader of Bethel Sozo, Author of Overcoming Fear, Shifting Atmospheres, Prayers, Declarations & Strategies, & co – author of SOZO, Saved, Healed, Delivered"

"My Heart's Garden is a must have book for every parent, grandparent, educator, pastor or mentor who desires children to grow deeper in their relationship with God and learn the truth of God's Word. With a catchy rhyme and whimsical illustrations, this powerful resource will help equip your children to overcome the lies of the enemy and fulfill their God given destinies."
-Brian Dixon, Author of Start with Your People and Co- Founder of Hope*Writers

"My friend Charity has written a great book for helping kids process feelings of shame and negative emotions, and replace them with truth about their identity in God's eyes."
- Joël Malm, Author of Love Slows Down

"The most important thing you can do as a parent is to teach your child to hear God's voice and to recognize the lies of the enemy. This book- My Heart's Garden by Charity Rios is a delightful tool every parent, grandparent, teacher and ministry worker must have to help the children in their lives know that God is real, and He has powerful truths He wants to share about who He has created them to be."
-Don and Suzanne Manning: Parents of 7 Jesus-loving-God-hearing children, Authors of Crazy Cool Family and Founders of Crazy Cool Family ministry.

"My Heart's Garden is a playful yet profound look at the lies we often believe, and will open up conversations that help kids step into their true identity."
-Christie Thomas, Author of Quinn's Promise Rock, Quinn Says Good – bye and Founder of Little Shoots, Deep Roots: Simplified Family Faith

DEDICATION

My 4 best boys: Caden, Finn, Zeke and Kian.   I wrote this book because the deepest prayer of my heart is for you to know Jesus, love the Word of God, and be free to fulfill the Divine destinies on your lives. I love you more than you will ever know! Love, Mama

The man of my dreams, Rene. Except for Jesus no one has ever believed in me the way you have. This book would not have happened without your belief and sacrifice. I love you so much. Love, Charity

C.R.

To my niece and nephews: Annabelle, Jacob, and John. You never fail to keep me young at heart and make me smile. Love you all.

DJ, my wonderful husband, thank you for always making me believe that I can do anything. I more than appreciate you, I love you.

A.B.

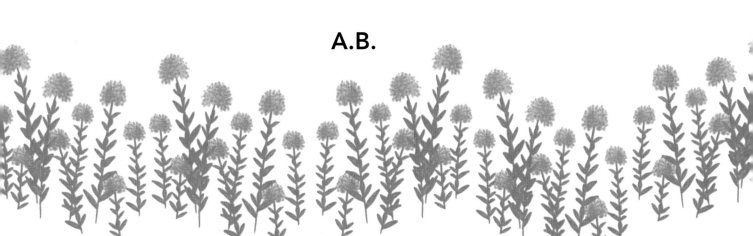

ION WAS A BOY,

FREE, BOLD, AND JOYFUL,

NOTHING HAD EVER

MADE HIS HEART SHAMEFUL.

ONE DAY THAT CHANGED
WHEN KIDS AT HIS SCHOOL,
YELLED OUT WORDS
LIKE, "YOU ARE A FOOL!"

AID HE WAS UGLY, DUMB, AND A KLUTZ,

"ZION, YOU DON'T BELONG WITH US!"

"YOUR NOSE IS TOO POINTY,

YOUR HAIR SMELLS LIKE DIRT,

YOU ALWAYS WEAR THE WRONG COLOR SHIRT."

EVERY DAY ZION'S THOUGHTS WOULD CONDEMN;
HE WAS WEIRD, UNWANTED, AND NOT ONE OF THEM.
AFTER A WHILE THEIR WORDS FELT TRUE,
HE WAS SAD AND LOST WITHOUT A CLUE.

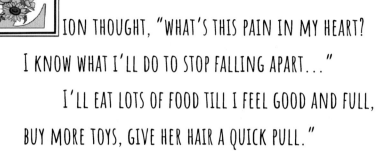

ION THOUGHT, "WHAT'S THIS PAIN IN MY HEART?
I KNOW WHAT I'LL DO TO STOP FALLING APART..."
    I'LL EAT LOTS OF FOOD TILL I FEEL GOOD AND FULL,
BUY MORE TOYS, GIVE HER HAIR A QUICK PULL."

 UT NOTHING COULD STOP

THE PAIN IN HIS HEART,

IT JUST GREW AND GREW

LIKE A SQUEEZED TIGHT FART.

HEN ZION WENT TO GRANNY,

TENDING HER GARDEN,

SHARING ALL

THE SAD THOUGHTS INSIDE HIM.

RANNY," ZION SAID,

"THERE ARE THOUGHTS IN MY HEAD, THEY ARE STRANGE AND DARK AND FILL ME WITH DREAD,

I CAN'T FORGET THEM EVEN THOUGH I TRY,

WHAT SHOULD I DO TO BID THEM GOOD-BYE?"

H MMM, I SEE" SHE SAID, LIFTING HER SHOVEL,
"WHEN DID THESE THOUGHTS START TO GIVE YOU SUCH TROUBLE?"
"WELL," ZION STAMMERED, TOE KICKING THE DIRT,
"IT STARTED WHEN KIDS SAID WORDS THAT HURT."

RYING SOFTLY,

HIS TEARS HITTING LEAVES, THEY CAME AS GRANNY BENT DOWN ON HER KNEES.

"ZION, THERE'S A GARDEN DEEP IN YOUR HEART.

FATHER GARDENER PLANTED IT, KNOWS EVERY PART."

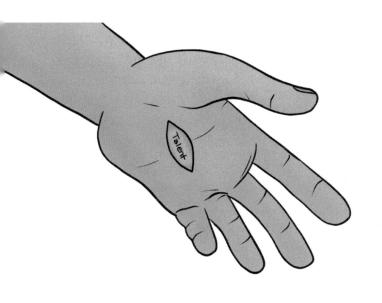

 e's put seeds inside
which make you unique.
            Your talents, dreams,
and your wild streak!"

HOSE THOUGHTS ARE LIES

FROM THE ONE WHO DECEIVES, THEY GROW THORNY TO CHOKE YOUR SEED LIKE A WEED."

Y PLANTS CAN'T GROW WITH A WEED UNATTENDED.

LIES WILT YOUR HEART UNLESS APPREHENDED."

"PULL OUT THAT WEED, IN YOUR HEART'S GARDEN.

ASK HIM TO WATER THE SEED THAT HE STARTED."

How can I pull it out?
It's so big and scary. The lie's been there so long,
it might even be hairy!"

SK FATHER GARDENER

      FOR COURAGE TO PULL THE WEED,

AND WATCH WHAT HE'LL BRING

      YOU TO WATER YOUR SEED."

ZION ASKED FATHER GARDENER,
"MAKE ME BRAVE AND BOLD!"
THEN, YELLING FIERCE AND LOUD,
THAT LIE GOT TOLD:

OU ARE A LIE—
GET OUT, OUT, OUT, OUT!!!!
THERE IS NO ROOM FOR THIS LIE
TO SPROUT!"

So I PULLED THE WEED UP
AND GOT THE LIE OUT, HOW CAN I KNOW
IF IT'S GONE BEYOND DOUBT?"

ERE'S WHAT YOU DO,"
GRANNY KNELT DOWN TO SHOW
        THE PLACE IN THE GROUND
WHERE THE WEED USED TO GROW
        "IN THIS EMPTY SPOT,
WHERE THE LIE DID RESIDE,
        YOU REPLACE IT WITH TRUTH
PLANTED INSIDE."

ATHER GARDENER WROTE THE TRUTH

THAT IS IN THIS LETTER,

READ IT NOW

AND YOU'LL KNOW HIM BETTER.

ION OPENED THE LETTER LONG AND DELICIOUS
AND SAVORED IT'S WORDS LIKE THE FINEST OF DISHES,
"ZION I HAVE THE ANSWER FOR YOUR HEART'S CURE,
ASK ME FOR THE TRUTH, AND I'LL GIVE IT FOR SURE."

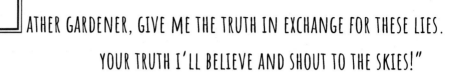

ATHER GARDENER, GIVE ME THE TRUTH IN EXCHANGE FOR THESE LIES.
YOUR TRUTH I'LL BELIEVE AND SHOUT TO THE SKIES!"

ZION SHARED THE TRUTH HE HAD HEARD
HIS HEART SOARING FREE,
LIKE A BEAUTIFUL BIRD.

RANNY," ZION SQUEALED,

"IT DOESN'T HURT ANYMORE!

FATHER GARDENER GAVE ME TRUTH

WHERE THE LIE WAS BEFORE."

HE SAID I WAS MADE
IN HIS IMAGE AND FORM,
CHOSEN AND CHERISHED
BEFORE I WAS BORN."

GRANNY, PATTING THE GROUND
            SURROUNDING THE FLOWER,
SAID, "YOUR HEART FULL OF TRUTH
            IS A SOURCE OF GREAT POWER."
"WITH THE LIE GONE,
            YOUR SEED CAN NOW FLOURISH
TALK WITH HIM,
            READ HIS WORDS TO STAY NOURISHED."

F A LIE COMES AGAIN
        AND YOUR HEART FEELS STRANGE,
GO TO FATHER GARDENER
        FOR THE BEAUTIFUL EXCHANGE."

E'LL GIVE TRUTH FOR THE LIES,
HIS PRESENCE FOR PAIN.
HE'S A DADDY WHO LOVES YOU
SENT HIS SON FOR YOUR GAIN.

A Special Note to Parents, Grandparents, Educators, Counselors, Pastors or Anyone reading this book!

Proverbs 4:23 (NASB) Instructs us to " Watch over your heart with all diligence, for from it flow the springs of life."

My Heart's Garden was written to help children learn from an early age how to watch over what their hearts are believing, so that they will experience the abundant life promised to us as Jesus followers. What we believe creates a roadmap for the choices we will make for the rest of our lives. False beliefs about God and ourselves are often born in traumatic or difficult events, such as when Zion is bullied at school. As parents, grandparents (and anyone investing in kids lives) we have the opportunity to help expose the lies of the enemy (Satan) and help our kids learn how to receive the truth available to them through God's Word (the Bible) and by hearing God's voice to them (the Rhema word of God, a word God speaks to an individual, see below for more info on hearing God's voice). This book is meant to be a helpful tool to uncover if there are places of pain where the enemy has used it as an opportunity to plant lies in our kid's minds and to get rid of those lies and replace them with the truth.

The simple yet profound process Zion goes through with Father Gardener is modeled after a process called "Tending your Heart." In simplest form, "Tending your Heart" is a Christian spiritual discipline so easy a child can do it and so life changing that it can radically transform an adult. I encourage you to not only help your child go through this process but also to practice it in your own devotional times with Jesus!

The best way to know if you are hearing God's voice is to make sure:
1. It aligns with the Word of God (the Bible)
2. It aligns with the Character of God (which we can learn and read about in the Bible)
3. It is encouraging. God's words to us never brings shame and condemnation, but instead lovingly bring us to repentance and call us forward into the abundant life He has for us!
(Romans 2:4)
>   ***If you aren't sure you can always talk with a trusted pastor or friend****

Guide your Children
As a parent you have the opportunity to guide your kids closer to Jesus in these conversations. There may often be times they say they aren't hearing anything or are hesitant to share. That's ok! Walking with Jesus is a journey and we have the high privilege and responsibility of guiding our children in their walks with Jesus. When your kids ask Jesus a question, you can also ask Jesus the question and be ready to share what you heard Him saying! I highly recommend always looking in the Bible for a scripture that also goes along with the truth you and/or your child are hearing.

How to Guide your Child through Tending your Heart:
Have you or your child write down or draw a picture of what they are hearing God say during this process.

Have your Child Ask:
- Father God, are there any lies I am believing about myself or you?
- Father God what is the truth?

Have your Child Pray:
- Father God, I am sorry for believing those lies (they can name the lie).
- Do you forgive me? (Yes! Our Father God always forgives us. This is a great chance to share about how Jesus died to take the punishment for all of our sins)

Have your Child Ask:
- Father God, what is the truth?

Have your Child Pray:
- Father God, thank you for this/these truth(s)

I recommend also finding a Bible verse that shares the truth your kids/you are hearing. This is a great verse to work on memorizing together!

Memorize the Word of God together
Want some FREE Scripture Memory verse cards, to memorize some scripture with your kids? Go to charityrios.com/myheartsgardenfreebies to download them!

One of the most powerful tools we can give our children is the Word of God memorized in their heart. My favorite way to memorize scripture with my kids is to come up with silly hand motions and practice the verse together! You will be amazed at how quickly kids can learn scripture (even my 2 year old is learning with us!) and you get the added benefit of memorizing or reviewing it with them. Here are some suggested memory verses to get you started, that address common struggles kids may have.

SALVATION
John 14:6 (NIV) Jesus answered, "I am the way and the truth and the life. No one comes to the Father except through me

IDENTITY
Psalm 139: 13-14 (ESV) For you formed my inward parts; you knitted me together in my mother's womb. I praise you, for I am fearfully and wonderfully made. Wonderful are your works; my soul knows it very well.
1 John 3:1 (NIV) See what great love the Father has lavished on us, that we should be called children of God! And that is what we are.

PEACE
2 Timothy 1:7 (ESV) for God gave us a spirit not of fear but of power and love and self-control.

FRUIT OF THE SPIRIT
Galations 5:22&23 (ESV) But the fruit of the Spirit is love, joy, peace, patience, kindness, goodness, faithfulness, gentleness, self-control; against such things there is no law.

Be sure to check out the My Heart's Garden Workbook, for an interactive and powerful way to teach your child the concepts of this book and deepen their personal relationship with Jesus. The workbook includes: 30 days of journal prompt questions for writing or drawing, coloring pages, Bible verse coloring page, crossword puzzle, scripture memory cards, and a maze.

ABOUT THE AUTHOR

Charity is a Jesus follower, Wife and Boy Mama to 4 of the wildest, and squishiest sets of dimpled cheeks. Most days you can find her top knottin' it, totin' potties and rollin' in the mini. The power of the gospel is her melody and unleashing women and children from captives into warriors is her passion.

She has a Masters in Higher Education and has been a Children's Pastor, Church Planter and Teacher. You can find Charity on Instagram @claritywithcharity, Facebook @CharityRios, Author or at charityrios.com.

ABOUT THE ILLUSTRATOR

Anna is an illustrator/ designer, Wife, and fun Aunt to three crazy kiddos. When she's not doodling up a storm, you can find her working in her other field of Interior Design creating beautiful interiors. She has a degree in fine art that she has used in every form of design she can think of and is looking for more. With her rocking husband DJ, the lead signer of Garden Music, creating art that reflects His design runs paramount in the Brennan household. You can find her on Instagram @annabrennandesigns.

SPECIAL THANKS

There are so many people who have supported this project in various ways, from donating funds, buying t-shirts, praying, and giving feedback. I may be credited as the author of this book, but God has truly used the Family of God, His Church, to bring forth this book into the world. A simple acknowledgement doesn't seem like enough, but please know how thankful I am for everything you have each invested into this project.
Forever Grateful,
Charity Rios

Jesus, My Savior, perfect and good Father God, and Wonderful Holy Spirit. You are worthy of ALL honor and glory and fame. May the world know your name instead of mine. Why you would choose a bleary eyed, pregnant Mama of 4 to bring this story into the world is beyond my understanding - but YOU have done it! Thank you for letting me partner with you in this great adventure, being faithful even when I have been faithless, and for making a way when there was no way.

Christie Thomas, for her story line and rhyme/rhythm editing expertise, along with her generous encouragement and author wisdom throughout the publishing process.

Cat Wise, for her grammatical editing expertise.

Lauren Mulvey, for being the first set of eyes on the text and providing such impactful prayer support for this project. You are this books "Auntie," your faith and love for this project has been pivotal in its completion.

Anna Brennan, for taking a risk on working with a first time, admittedly clueless author on your first children's book illustration project. You have been so gracious and a dream to work with on this project.

The McGrath Family, for your support of this project. Thank you for listening to Jesus and being quick to obey.

The Tucker Family, thank you for your support of this book, you are a family marked by humility and generosity.

My team of Mom and Teacher experts giving feedback on the book. You are each treasured friends. Your wisdom, input and encouragement through this process meant more than you know: Katy Pleasant, Gloria Joecks, Jenna Taylor, Lauri Evans, Lauren Mulvey, Ashlee Hardy, Christy Martin, Danielle Adair, Doxie Wilson, Arlina Pletcher, Amanda Buenger, Carisse Lowry, Heather Puceck, Ellen Curnette, Gillean Wade, Allison Flippen, Alex Donaldson, Chelsey Russell, Maggie Mc Grath, & Anna Decker

My Husband, Rene Rios Jr, for your encouragement & sacrifice throughout this journey. Also thank you for your incredible website building and techie skills which have saved me from many a disaster!

My Mom (Rachel Joecks) and late Dad (Larry Joecks), for instilling in me a love of the Word of God.

My Brother, Victor Joecks and sister in law, Gloria Joecks, not only are you family but you are both some of my favorite people on the planet. Thank you for always believing in me and rarely letting me win at Cataan.

Katy Pleasant, nobodies' cuter than you! Thank you for always believing I would publish a book and for saving me from make - up pyramid schemes, listening to the world's longest voice memos and being a friend that sticks closer than a sister. (Proverbs 18:24)

Friends, Family and some complete Strangers that bought a t-shirt to help produce this book. Your investment in eternity will be rewarded and I believe with more than just a cute tee, Thank you! (listed as typed in on the purchase orders)

Don Manning, Chelsey Russell, Terry Mcgrath, Katy Pleasant, Zachary R., Christy M., Gloria Joecks, Danielle Adair, Carolina Barrero, Lauri Evans, Arlina P., Jenna Taylor, Sarah Best, Tersea Lynn Rios, Anthony Gardea, Laura Smith, Beth R., Katherine Newsom, Dj B., Jay N., Shelly Templin, Gillean Wade, Carly Rush, Ellen Curnutte, Sarah K, Joy Hale, Maddie R., Amanda Griffith, Sarah A, Sherry Chao, Zachary R, Celeste A, Shirley F, Beth Medley, Julie A, Alex D, Eunice Ellis, Rachel Joecks Christi P, Tamara W, Adam Conkle, Josh B, Brittany Rose, Lauren M, Laurie G, John P, Anthony A Pucek, Anna R. D, Hannah T, Carisse L, Nicole L, Sheryl J, Ashton Alcorn, Matthew S, Kristin B, Beth W, Chelsea T, Sarah R, Gloria M, Caroline Bosley, Amanda Thorn, Renee B, Rachel F.

We would love to see your pics with the book! Use #myheartsgardenkidsbook and be sure to tag @claritywithcharity and @annabrennandesigns in your Instagram post. Or tag on Facebook: @charityrios,author.

For FREE My Heart's Garden Coloring Sheets and further resources to help your children deepen their relationship with Jesus visit charityrios.com/myheartsgardenfreebies.

Be sure to check out the My Heart's Garden Workbook (available on Amazon). Designed with interactive activities, beautiful illustrations to color, & journal questions for parents or mentors to guide your child through, this workbook will help kids deepen their relationship with Jesus.

Made in United States
Orlando, FL
11 December 2021